Reflec

H.D.W. Loten

&

R.E. Loten

Reflections was first published in 2021.
This edition published by *Castle Priory Press.*

ISBN 9798767974351

Contents

Walking up Rough Tor
H.D.W. Loten

Between a series of trees, a bridge.
On its right a clear lake,
beset on all sides by regal purple plants.
Along the large hill, horses and sheep
graze freely ‘cross lines of small stones.
In a few yards a small stream
runs away from the lake,
towards the trees
and the other lake.

Over the bridge,
a long winding path of stones and
grass trails up to rocky heights,
over thirteen hundred feet skyward.
Shoes are threatened by dugouts
in the bog by the streams.

Looking north to the hilltop
there are hundreds,
if not thousands of rocks, stones and boulders,
turning the tor into a formidable fortress.
The sheer number
of littered stones is astonishing.
They look like the casualties
that surround the castles
in the aftermath of a major engagement –
all that is missing are the banners.

Zigzagging, trench-like grass paths
separate the rocks as it begins to get steeper.
Behind, a steadily steepening slope is
guarded by an army of green grass,
crisp brown ferns and
other types of fauna.
Dotted with moss covered rocks.
A battlefield of plants
against stones.
The plants are winning.

Looking again at the hill,
piles of man-sized boulders
are scattered across it.
A tower had fallen from the tor,
but it's flanking walls still stand defiant.

It is a formidable climb,
dotted with rabbit holes and sharp edges.

From three-quarters up
you can see the
house-sized cairns on Little Rough Tor.
To the northwest some misty mountains.

At the rocky crest, is more of the same,
just windier.
In all directions there are
more pockets of trees and
clouded hills,
paths and roads.
Many are shrouded
in shade cast by the large
cloud formations and the sun.

It's big.
I sit.
I breathe.

Drum of Passchendaele
H.D.W. Loten
(originally published in "Tattoo - Makarelle')

Most think Hell is a huge fire
a boiling inferno of blood
But here we know, Hell is a brown wasteland;
a machine gun that echoes through the night;
mortars firing across scarred fields
that once wore green,
now scorched beneath trench and wire.

And they march their feet to the beat.

Filth is the norm,
Slurry and sludge drip off everything
and pile onto the rising decay.
Roads and farms: all are gone
Is there glory to be won?

And they heave to the hi-hat.

Know, many will suffer.
Know, many mutilated.
Know, many will die.
How many shall they take?
And the dusk falls,
And the raids begin
And the killing carries on.

And they scream to the snare.

Clocks crawl in the light of day
The night covers the sky like a cloth
Time picks up, it moves in a blur
and the dreams of home flutter
Like blossoms from trees as they tumble to the ground,
a gentle breeze that fills an empty heart.
A fire, long extinguished, relights.
Flowers of yellow, red, white, and blue
all billowing like smoke in the wind.

And they stumble to the cymbal.

Know, many have suffered.
Know, many are maimed.
Know, many have died.
No glory will ever be won.
And the dawn breaks,
And the battles begin
And the killing carries on.

And they slog on to the toms.

A forlorn Tommy pushes on,
waist-high in mud.
Stuck in the trenches.
Stuck in the slush.
And the men crawl
And the brass hats plan
Will the killing carry on?

And they march their feet to the beat
And they heave to the hi-hat
And they scream to the snare
And they stumble to the cymbal
And they toil on to the toms
And they die
to the Drum
of Passchendaele.

Fiercely and Faithfully
H.D.W. Loten

For His Holiness.
For the might of His Kingdom.
For the Cross of Christ.

Saint Peter's Basilica floats
on a sea of dead Germans.
Battle rages in the Graveyard of Teutons
And the 189 stand

For His Holiness.
For the might of His Kingdom.
For the Cross of Christ.

Their Captain had drowned in that ocean.
Hopeless. Futile. Outnumbered
but not outmatched. On they go,
massacred where they stand

For His Holiness.
For the might of His Kingdom.
For the Cross of Christ.

Scarper! The order to flee
straight down di Borgio.
Silver flashes on the way to the Castel.
And the 42 stand

For His Holiness.
For the might of His Kingdom.
For the Cross of Christ.
Acriter et Fideliter.

Eagle One, Eagle Two
R.E. Loten
(originally published in "Twisted Tales – Makarelle')

I need to write this down. If I don't, I'll forget it happened. Forget it was ever more than a story. I'm a writer by trade, but the truth is far stranger than any fiction I could ever invent. Isn't it always though?

I walked past the hotel and shuddered. They were doing it again. Looking at me. I mean, obviously they weren't. How could they? They were made of stone. Stone can't look at you. So why did it feel like that's exactly what they were doing? I gave myself a metaphorical shake. They were just decorations. Nothing more than stone statues designed to make the hotel entrance look grander. And as for the one on the roof, well that was pure eighteenth century patriotism at its very best. The hotel was originally a mansion, built by the wealthy mayor of the town in the days of George III and the architecture was typical of the grandiose posturing such people preferred, with eagles guarding the gates, Britannia on the roof and an abundance of columns and white stucco adorning the smart red brickwork. Everything about it screamed wealthy, imperial Britain. It was a truly beautiful building, but those statues gave me the creeps. I'd only lived in Launceston a few weeks and already I didn't like walking past them at night. Deep down, I knew it was only my over-active imagination having 'fun' with my nerves, but still.

As I reached the opening in the wall which gave access to the outdoor dining area, a woman dressed in black and with a veil covering her face, passed me on the other side of it. A faint waft of lavender drifted behind her and the scent made me turn, as I always do, to inhale it again. It's such a soothing smell: it reminds me of my grandmother.

The woman had disappeared. She'd had no time to enter the bar or the hotel. She was just… gone.

Not giving myself time to think, I turned on my heel and almost sprinted through the old gatehouse and onto the green of the castle grounds beyond. *I was mistaken. There was no woman. Or if there was, she was simply hidden behind something.* The sun was beating down and I'd been busy all morning building furniture. I was just hungry. That had to be it. Just my tired, hungry brain misinterpreting the signals it had been sent.

I bought myself a pasty from the shop on the High Street and sat by the war memorial to eat it. I know, I know… I sat in the sun in Cornwall eating a Cornish pasty, but honestly, I don't care. The ones from Malcolm Barnecutt's are so nice it's worth being a walking (or in this case, sitting) cliché. I closed my eyes, allowing the glorious weather to chase away the last of the fear that insisted on lurking in the furthest recess of my mind. I scolded myself. How could I have let my imagination run away with me so badly? I'd been in the hotel for several drinks and a meal. I'd spoken to the owners, who were lovely by the way, and on not one of these occasions had there been any hint of ghostly old women. In the short time I'd been in Launceston, I'd realised that one thing the locals were always happy to tell you about was any hint of a ghost. Even if they claim to be completely sceptical themselves, the Cornish know their local history and the accompanying ghosts and I'm pretty sure that one of their favourites past-times is scaring the emmets. Technically, I no longer count as an emmet as I live here and am doing my best to learn the language, but I'm also clearly not Cornish born and bred, so I'm probably still fair game when it comes to the spooky stories. My next door neighbour certainly takes great delight in sharing them with me.

Wiping the last flakes of pastry from the corners of my mouth, I stretched and rose from my seat. For a moment I debated whether to take the longer route back to my flat, past the church and down the narrow path that ran alongside it. It was steeper but it would mean I didn't have to walk past the hotel again. Deciding I was being ridiculous, I jammed my sunglasses firmly back up my nose and headed towards the castle.

'Dydh da.'

Two voices made me jump as the contrast between the shadowy coolness of the gatehouse and the brilliant sunlight momentarily disorientated me. I squinted at the two small figures before my brain processed what they'd said.

'Dydh da.' I smiled apologetically. 'That's about the extent of my Cornish, I'm afraid.'

The two fair haired boys grinned at me.

'Emmet?'

'No, I live here. It's the first time I've heard anyone speaking Cornish though. I'm guessing you must be local. Are you fluent?'

The boys nodded and broke into a stream of Cornish, taking it in turns to gabble away at me.'

I laughed and held up my hands. 'Very impressive boys, but I didn't understand a word!'

They looked at each other and smiled.

'You saw her, didn't you?'

I frowned. 'Who?'

'The old lady.'

I felt my feet root themselves to the ground even as I felt the urge to flee.

'We were sitting up there and we saw you react.'

'Did she say anything?'

'Did she look old?'

I held up my hands. 'I thought I'd imagined her.'

'No, she's real. Well, as real as a ghost can be. She's the old owner's mother. He killed himself, you know. She haunts the house looking for him.'

That caught my attention. It certainly hadn't been in the potted history of the hotel I'd been given.

'That's terrible.'

The boys looked at each other again.

'They say it's because he had his heart broken.'

'He fell in love with a woman and they got engaged. Then she just disappeared. Left him all alone and he drowned himself in the Kensey down by the packhorse bridge.'

I had a feeling I was being wound up. At that point the river is barely more than a stream. The boys seemed to sense my scepticism and hastened to assure me of the truth of their tale.

'Apparently, he just lay down with his face in the water one night. They found him the next day.'

Poor lady, I thought. I said goodbye to the boys and continued down the hill, resisting the urge to check if the eagles were still watching me. Just before I turned the corner I glanced back. The boys were gone, but the eagles were there, heads turned away from each other, watching the hill in both directions. I walked quickly round the bend and back down the road to my flat.

A few days later, I decided to go for a drink. It was a beautiful summer's evening and the view from the hotel terrace was glorious at sunset. I'd been cooped up inside all day and felt I deserved a treat. I walked slowly up the hill, anticipating the cold notes of blueberries and raspberries in the Eagle One gin I'd promised myself if I stayed at my desk all day.

As I sat watching the sun sink slowly behind the trees, I noticed a dark figure alone at a table in the corner of the terrace. For a moment, I looked at my glass: it was still almost full. I looked over again. She was still there. As I processed this, she caught my eye and nodded an acknowledgment. Tentatively I smiled and she beckoned me over. I picked up my drink and took the few steps across the terrace.

'Do I present such a fearsome picture?' she asked.

Her face was deeply lined with age, but now I'd established she was flesh and blood, it held no horrors for me and I shook my head, half-laughing at myself.

'Not in the least. It's only that I caught sight of you a few days ago and you seemed to just vanish and then I was told you were a ghost. A joke, I realise, but it was a bit of a shock to see you sitting there.'

Her answering laugh was dry and brittle, like the rustle of old paper.

'I'm old but I'm not dead yet.'

'My imagination runs away with me sometimes. I'm a writer you see, so it's mostly an advantage, but it does mean I'm easy to frighten. I don't particularly like statues at the best of times and this place is old and it's Cornwall and there's ghosts everywhere. You get the idea! My neighbour thinks it's great fun to torment me with ghost stories.'

'And was it your neighbour who told you I was a ghost?'

I shook my head. 'No. That particular gem came courtesy of two little boys. I bumped into them just outside the gates and they took great delight in telling me the story of the old lady whose son had killed himself, because the woman he loved left him. They said you were his mother still haunting the hotel and looking for him.'

My smile faded away as I took in the expression on her face. Her hand clamped over mine, her grip surprisingly strong given her frail appearance.

'That's no story. My son did kill himself many years ago for that reason, but there's none left alive now who would remember. What did the boys look like?'

'Very like each other. Blonde curly hair. Twins maybe?'

The hand gripping mine convulsed and she made a choking sound.

'One of them had a scar on his cheek.'

Now she mentioned it, I remembered the mark clearly and I nodded.

'That's right.'

'You can't possibly have spoken to them. Those boys are dead.'

I stared at her, feeling the perspiration slide down my back.

'Dead?' I echoed.

'Murdered by a madwoman over a hundred years ago.' I took an unsteady sip from my glass as she continued. 'Local witch. Didn't like the fact her beloved son had taken up with a woman who already had two children. He didn't care, loved them like they were his own, but the witch knew what the woman was really like. On the surface she was loving and kind, but the witch knew. She knew the woman was only pretending. Her son was wealthy. Owned a beautiful house. The woman had nothing. The son wasn't a good-looking boy and he was quiet and shy. Some said it was because his mother had too firm a hand over him. She'd cast a spell on him to keep him close to her. The spell wasn't strong enough though and he fell for the woman. His mother was mad with jealousy. The woman was going to take her son away from her. She was going to hurt him. The witch gave her fair warning. She told the woman she knew what she was about. The woman protested of course: said she truly loved the witch's son. But the witch knew better. She had to protect her son. She cursed the woman and her sons, but the curse went wrong. When her son saw the new statues on the house he knew what his mother had done and he swore he would never forgive her. She told him he was overreacting, that she'd done it to protect him. The woman had never really loved him, but he wouldn't listen. The witch was worried, so she renewed the spell that kept them bound together, but her son escaped and they found him the next morning, face down in the river.'

I swear I didn't make a sound, but she must have felt my hand twitch, for she tightened her grip on it.

'The spell worked though. The statues remain so the son remains, still wanting to be close to his love. And because the son remains, so must the mother. I've been here a long time, my dear and will be here a while longer.'

She released my hand abruptly and left me alone at the table. The hotel's owner suddenly appeared at my elbow.

'Are you alright?' he asked. 'Mrs Kendall can be a little intense sometimes, but she's generally harmless. Has she been telling you ghost stories about this place?'

I nodded. 'Who is she?'

He frowned. 'She came with the hotel when we bought it. She's a permanent resident and has a suite on the top floor. We only ever really see her for meals.'

I handed him my now empty gin glass, feeling the need to return home to the safety of my flat. Had she been telling me the truth or was she, like my neighbour, entertaining herself at my expense?

As I walked past the hotel entrance I glanced up at Britannia, then my eye fell on the eagles. I stared at the nearest one. It gazed back, unblinking.

Stalingrad

H.D.W. Loten

Red in the houses,
Grey in the streets.
The volcano erupts
As bombs burn the homes.

A monochrome of suffering.

Grey.
The colour of our sky.
The colour of our burg.
The colour of our death.
Red.
The colour of the fields.
The colour of the streets.
The colour of the buildings.

Grey in the streets.
Planes covered the heavens,
Now we cover the ground.

Red in the houses,
We hold in our rooms,
and we hold in our buildings.

Grey in the streets.
We are slaughtered
by this army of Red steel.

Red in the houses,
Together, we prevail for
the glory of the Motherland.

Grey in the streets.
Together, we die with
the glory of the Fatherland.

Red in the houses,
Grey in the streets
The volcano calms
But the fires still blaze.

A monochrome of death.

The Red fell in the houses.
The Grey fell in the streets.
They fell in the sky.
They fell in the river.
They fell in the city.

They fell for the city.

On This Day
H.D.W. Loten

On this day,
Man made Hell worse.

A hill on the ground.
A hill with gunpowder.
A hill in the sky.
A hill by the sun.
A hill in free fall.
A hill under the ground.
A hill of graves.

On this day,
Man made Hell worse.

An ocean of silence and simplicity. An ocean
of waves and tides. An
ocean of suddenness.
An ocean of surprise.
An ocean of noise and
suffering. An ocean of
screaming metal.
An ocean consumed by death.
An object beneath the ocean.
An object of death.

On this day,
Man made Hell worse.

A cloud of the land.
A cloud of pepper.
A cloud of pineapple.
A cloud of asphyxiation.
A cloud of blindness.
A cloud of burning.
A cloud of death.

On this day,
Man made Hell worse.

A beast that breathes
no air. A beast
that has no flesh.
A beast that knows
no mercy, simply
death. A beast that spits
fire and fury. A beast that
screams then shatters.
A beast with wheels.
A beast of fuel.
A beast of steel.

Welcome Home To Cornwall

R.E. Loten

(originally published on the Shaftesbury Tree Festival website)

My foot inches closer to the floor as my car devours the miles of the A30. Ahead of me, just coming into view I can see them. One hundred and forty beech trees grouped together in a little copse at the top of a hill. 'Welcome home,' they say. Will I be welcome though? Have I become an emmet in my absence? When I left, approaching them from the opposite direction, I noticed a single tree further down the hill. It looked as though the others had all turned their backs on it because it had left their group to explore new pastures. I was excited for it then. It was off to new adventures. Now I just felt sorry for it.

I thought my life was beginning when I left Cornwall, but five years later, here I am, driving down the same old road, returning to the county of my birth. It's an old story, told for ever more in romantic comedies: girl meets boy, girl and boy fall in love, girl follows boy back to the big city, girl and boy marry. Boy dies. Yeah, maybe that last bit isn't quite as funny. I could have stayed there, I suppose, I had a job, friends, a life. None of it meant anything though. Not without him. And so I decided to move back home. Not to my parents' house – I couldn't do that again. But back to Cornwall at least. Somewhere I can heal.

I risk another glance at the trees and I feel something settle over me. A sense of calm I haven't felt since Tim died. There's something so reassuringly solid about them. They've been there all my life, welcoming us home whenever we went on holiday. Someone would always say, 'Almost home now,' whenever we saw them. We weren't of course – there was still almost an hour of driving left, but we were on the final stretch at least.

The trees are famous in their own right now. Nobody truly knows why they were planted there, but they've been welcoming people to Cornwall for over a hundred years. They've been immortalised in paintings and prints and sold by the thousand all across the county under different titles. Trees are said to have great healing qualities and to some extent it's true – I've walked miles through woodlands in the last few months. These ones are different though. They're more than just trees. For me they're simply, home.

The Ones Who Die
H.D.W. Loten

We are the ones who did our best.
We are the ones who are vaunted.
We are the ones who cannot rest.
We are the ones who are haunted.
We are the ones who were blindly led.
We are the ones whose minds are dead.

The sole survivor of his Platoon,
He became a man in a day.
The boy within lost all his tune
The moment he joined the fray.
There's no reward for him to reap
Now fallen comrades haunt his sleep.

The pilot falling from the sky
Seeing heaven's light
As he tumbled from up high,
Abandoning his flight.
His mind once active, today is meek
Now he's forgotten how to speak.

The driver of a burning landship,
Was stuck in its blazing shell.
The congealing blood continued to drip
In that dreaded inferno from Hell.
The decision to serve, he would regret
Now he finds he can't forget.

The POW in a camp far from home,
Now freezing half to death.
He wouldn't have signed up, had he known,
This would be his last breath.
His face so thin, no longer pink
Now he's worn down, he cannot think.

We are the ones who did our best.
We are the ones who are vaunted.
We are the ones who cannot rest.
We are the ones who are haunted.

We can't sleep.
We can't speak.
We can't forget.
We can't think.
We can only dread.
We can only dream of being dead.

The Helter Skelter
H.D.W. Loten

Look at all the lonely people,
I'm crying after a hard day's night,
Not everyone has got her,
Ma belle, Michelle.

I want to hold her hand,
She likes to drive my car,
through the Norwegian Woods
and back into the USSR.

I wanted her so bad,
We went down to Penny Lane,
She took me to Sergeant Pepper's
and I said something wrong.

Tried to see it my way,
Misunderstanding, all we saw,
That Tuesday afternoon was never ending.
Shoot me.

While I gently wept,
Here came the sun,
If I was lonely, I could talk to her,
"Let it be" she said.

No one compares to you,
What did I know?
Oh, darling,
I feel fine.

Battle of Breitenfeld
H.D.W. Loten

A decade of war.
Slowly returning to peace,
yet the Lion still roars,
Gustavus Adolphus calls.
Two decades now remain.

Shells scream.
Mist fills the air
with the noxious stench of death.
It surrounds them
with the regular,
but randomised drum of death.

The end of the old.
The rise of the north,
reaching south.
For the Yellow and Blue.
A defence of the faith.

Flashes of light
fills up the short horizon
Blasts swing around them
and shimmer like a million eyes,
spotlighted onto their faces.

The rise of the new.
The fall of the south,
fleeing from the north.
Black and Yellow.
A defence of empire or faith?

Muskets on both sides spray ahead,
firing as if they were water,
falling into an infinitely large cup.
It overflows to form pools of sorrow,
Among a typhoon wave of man and beast.
They howl at the opposite side.

The Saxons cry out,
Gott mit Uns!
the call of death
to the Catholics.

Maroon masks serrate their faces,
pools of sweat
condense across freezing foreheads.
Bodies creak.
Cracking under the immense strain
as hundreds of men hold their banners aloft.

The Catholics cry out,
Father Tilly!
a wavering call,
A final breath.

Bullets bring their cold
hard embrace to a shrivelling life force.
The Kiss of Death,
the only form of love to be found.

The Lion from the North,
stories of the prophetic return.
September 7th , a day of fear.
The Imperial Eagle falters.

Germans drift,
Spaniards stumble,
Catholics flail,
as their minds open up.

The Swedes cry out,
Gott mit Uns!
the call of death
to the Empire.

Cannons bloated out
as their strings were lit
and they flew across the battle
tumbling like a heeling eagle
before disgorging scraps of steel.

The end of the old.
The rise of the Lion,
reaching south.
For the Yellow and Blue.
An attack on the Eagle.

Pellets of iron
and lead zoom
through the sky,
like a lion on the hunt.

The Protestants cry out,
Gott mit Uns!
the call of praise
to Gustavus Adolphus II.

A Dymond In The Rough

R.E.Loten

It's cold and the sound of the scuttling rats competes with the drumbeat of the water dripping from the ceiling. I don't know how long I've been here. Days? Weeks? I don't think it's months, but I can't be sure. They say it becomes easier to bear the death of a loved one with time, so however long it's been, it's not been long enough to make the fact of her death any easier to bear. I miss her. She was warm and kind, my Charlotte, with a smile that could light up the darkest winter night. It's funny, but I can still feel her here with me. It's comforting in a way, I suppose – not being alone I mean – but she doesn't belong here. She was a moor girl, wild and free. She shouldn't be cooped up in here. Not like me. I deserve to be here. I killed her.

Oh, not in the way they think I did. It wasn't me who slit her throat. I don't like to think about that too much. She had such a pretty throat; slender and white like a swan's. I used to like kissing it: my kisses left little red flowers where she blushed at the touch. They were delicate blooms though, not like the crimson ribbon she wore that last day. I could never have hurt her. Not like that. But I did though, didn't I? I hurt her that day. That's why she left me. That's how she ended up in Roughtor Ford. I should have known it was too good to last. She was always too good for me in spite of what she said. Pretty maid like her should have been with someone who could walk without limping, whose back was straight, whose face was as handsome as hers. I never could tell what she saw in me. Folks said it was 'cause I had a little money, but I knew that weren't the reason. She weren't like that. Oh she knew the value of money like the rest of us do, but I didn't have enough of it to compensate for the rest of me. If that'd been the reason she was after me, she'd have gone with Prout the first time he asked her. He's better looking than I am and he's got more cash. No, she were with me because she wanted to be, no matter how hard that is for me to fathom.

I'd cut myself shaving that morning and when I met her at the back door, that was the first thing she noticed.

'Oh Matthew! It's all on your collar.' She dabbed at it with her handkerchief. 'It's all dried on. Give it to me when we come home and I'll wash it for you, see if I can get the stain out.'

She sounded exasperated. It wasn't the best start to our day off and I'd wanted it to go so well today. Today had to be perfect because that's what she deserved. I put my hand in my pocket, seeking the reassurance of the object concealed within. *It will all be well*, I told myself. *Just screw up your courage and do it man.*

We walked over the moors all morning, Charlotte and me. We didn't talk much, but then we often didn't. It was enough for me just to be out there with her, holding her hand, knowing she was mine. We sat on our usual rock for lunch – it was a flattish one right at the top of Roughtor – and sat in silence looking out over the rough track towards Brown Willy. It was peaceful and beautiful and then I ruined it. Unable to find the words to express what I felt, I simply tapped my darling girl on the shoulder and held the ring out to her. I hadn't expected her to say yes so quickly, but she threw her arms around me and kissed me. That was when it all went wrong.

'I think you should leave the farm,' I said.

She stared at me for a moment before replying. 'Why? If I carry on working we can save more.'

'I've enough that you don't have to work.'

'But I want to. If I keep on for a bit longer and save, then with your money we could maybe buy a little smallholding just for us.'

'I still think you should leave.'

'Why?' she demanded. 'What are you not telling me?'

'He's got his eye on you and I don't like it.'

'John? Don't be daft.'

'Not John. *Him.* Prout. Don't pretend you haven't noticed.'

'Lots of men look at me Matthew. Doesn't mean I've any interest in them though, does it?'

'Lots of men? Exactly how many men *have* you got sniffing around you?'

She laughed. 'Hundreds! Thousands maybe. But why would I want any of them when I've got you?'

Jealousy made me stubborn and I scowled at her. 'I still think you ought to leave. It ain't right him making eyes at you when he knows you're my girl.'

'Your girl am I? I'll have you know Matthew Weeks, I don't belong to anyone. Just 'cause you put a ring on my finger doesn't mean I'm yours to order around.'

She stood up and brushed angry fingers down the green stripes of her dress.

'Charlotte don't be angry. It worries me, that's all.'

'I can take care of myself. I've been doing it all my life.'

I looked away and bit my lip. 'You haven't seen the way he looks at you when you're not looking at him. I don't like it, Charlotte.'

'He got the message that I wasn't interested. Stop worrying.'

Of course my worries immediately increased. 'What do

you mean? Why did you have cause to tell him?'

'He cornered me and put his hands on me. I stuck my knee…' She gestured towards my most sensitive area and I winced a little, in spite of my rising anger. 'I threatened to tell his aunt what her precious nephew had tried to do, but he got in first and told her I'd tried it on with him. That's why she let me go. I threatened to tell everyone what had happened so she said I could stay for a few weeks until I got a new situation.'

'Why didn't you tell me? I would have helped.'

'No you wouldn't. You'd have lost your head and thumped him and then we'd both have been out of a job.'

She began to walk away from me and I panicked. 'Where are you going?'

'Over to Blisland. Going to see if I can get a job there seeing as how my fiancé doesn't trust me around certain other men. I'll stay at Maggie's tonight and go there in the morning.'

Her tone was harsh, but the softness of her expression made me think I'd not offended her too badly.

'Shall I come with you?'

'No. It would only draw attention. If I can't get work there I'll go to your sister and find work in Plymouth somewhere. If you don't hear from me come down there next week.'

'I'll not stay there,' I told her. 'I can't. Not now.'

She came back, bent down and kissed my forehead. 'You're a dear man. That's exactly why I didn't tell you.' She pulled me to my feet. 'Go and cool off somewhere before you go back to the farm.' She opened her mouth as if to add something further then closed it again.

'Go on,' I urged her. ' There should be no secrets between us if we're to marry. What is it?'

'You don't…' she bit her lip and studied her feet for a

moment. 'You don't think I led him on, do you? That what he did was my fault.'

'Well you did smile at him an awful lot,' I said. It was meant to be a gentle tease, to reassure her that I didn't. But as usual, it came out all wrong and I knew from the hurt expression that creased her face that I'd messed everything up. Before I could say anything she walked away from me, the fringe of her red shawl streaming out behind her as she stamped down the hill. I hoped the fact she hadn't returned my ring meant we were still to marry, though I feared I was taking too much for granted. Cursing myself, I trudged back across the moor towards the farm.

That was the last time I saw her.

The following week I went to my sister's as planned, having told Mrs Peter that Charlotte had left and making it clear I knew why. She wasn't there when I arrived; my sister hadn't seen her. I knew then we would never marry. One careless sentence had lost her. By the time they came to arrest me, I knew they'd found her body and I no longer cared what happened to me. Without her I had nothing. Was nothing. So when Prout came to see me with my confession, I knew it was him. He killed my Charlotte. Mrs Peter knew half the countryside and even if I'd wanted to protest my innocence, no one would have believed my word against theirs. I signed the confession without even reading it. I couldn't have done anyway. Charlotte tried to teach me to read and write, but I never mastered more than my own name. I was content to allow justice to chart its own course. To my way of thinking, even if it was Prout who struck the final blow that robbed Charlotte and me of our future, it was my carelessness that put her in his way. I can only guess at what happened that day. Perhaps he met Charlotte as she was on her way to Blisland and tried again to take from her what she'd so stoutly defended at the farm. I don't know if he succeeded, but I know my Charlotte, she'd have put up a fight to the end. Maybe that's why he killed her; he had to stop her telling everyone. She would have done as well. Utterly fearless my girl was. Doesn't matter in the end. We can't change the past. I hope this will atone for what I did though. That in accepting my fate, I'll find her afterwards and we'll be together as we planned.

The cell door opens and I lift my head, blinking at the sudden change in illumination. I rise slowly, my joints stiff with cold and damp and I begin my slow shuffle towards the light.

Gallipoli
H.D.W. Loten

Churchill promised victory,
A single Company to beat,
The Dardanelles are weak,
With the rapid march of our feet.
A fortnight to capture the meek.

Shattered, young men are lost,
Promises of victories mere myths,
Bodies strewn on the beach,
Underneath Gallipoli's cliffs,
Positions, they never did reach.

Diggers pour from the Clyde,
Diggers fall in the sand,
Men die where they stand.
Diggers digging in.

Kiwis storming beaches,
Kiwis falling from hills,
There are no promised thrills.
Kiwis digging in.

Jackos inside their forts,
Jackos thunder the beach,
The shells begin to screech.
Jackos digging in.

Tommies going over,
Tommies are strafed by all,
Crows circle as they fall.
Tommies digging in.

Sepoys slogging forward,
Sepoys flailing on through,
            Red faces are now blue.
Sepoys digging in.

Newfies holding the line,
Newfies launching attacks,
            Orders not to fall back.
Newfies digging in.

Poilu scaling the cliffs,
Poilu in futile hope,
            Not one survived the slope.
Poilu digging in.

Legions coming ashore,
Legions joining the fight,
            Many see their last light.
Legions digging in.

Allies retreat offshore,
Allies without their bark,
            Retreating under cover of dark.
Allies, don't dig in.

Shattered, young men are lost,
Promises of victories mere myths,
Bodies strewn on the beach,
            Underneath Gallipoli's cliffs.
Positions, they never did reach.

Shattered, men aren't unearthed,
Promises of death were not myths,
Bodies strewn on the beach,
            Underneath Gallipoli's cliffs.
Positions, they could never reach.

An Unnamed Soldier
H.D.W. Loten

Goodbye mother,
It's tough to die,
When all the lights begin to fade,
Will you look at the birds that fly?

Hello darkness,
Is this all real?
My life essence is bleeding out,
Is this pain how death is to feel?

Goodbye father,
It's tough to die,
When all the lights begin to fade,
Will you look down on me and sigh?

Hello coldness,
When will it end?
Battle's over, yet I'm still here,
Will all of these wounds ever mend?

Goodbye sister,
It's tough to die,
When all the lights begin to fade,
Will you look to the heavens and cry?

Hello Reaper,
You are now here.
Was my life lost for a good cause?
Will any of this make me fear?

Goodbye brother,
It's tough to die,
When all the lights begin to fade,
Will you look up and say goodbye?

Hello darkness.
This is now it.
Nothing remains and I'm not here,
To your cold embrace I submit.

Goodbye Cruel World,
It's tough to die,
When all the lights begin to fade,
Will you look to the big blue sky?

Goodbye mother,
It's tough to die,
When all the lights begin to fade,
Will you look at the birds that fly?

The Cathedral of the Moor

R.E. Loten

I trail my hand in the stream, watching as the water bubbles and plays over my pale skin. What am I to do? He says not to worry, but how can I not? I don't want this child growing inside me. Mother tells me it's the beginning of a new life, but she's wrong. It's the ending of one. I was happy working at the vicarage until she pushed me forward. How could I have known what he was like? I'd barely spoken to him in the time I'd been there. What would a kitchen maid have had to say to a vicar? Mother thinks he will marry me. 'He's a man of God,' she says, 'How can he do otherwise?' She believes I will become mistress of the vicarage, but how can I? How could I face those faces every Sunday? They would know who I was. There may be a ring on my finger but they'd know I was just Jane, the kitchen maid who lay down for her master. Or worse – an upstart who seduced a good man into sin.

Mother might be right. He is a good man. He is gone to get a marriage license. Mother is cock-a-hoop. She plans to run this house. Her scheme is bearing fruit but she will ruin him and he won't even realise it. She's already dropping hints that I was less than willing. Nothing could be further from the truth. I had no thought of him that she did not put there, but when she brought me to him everything changed. I saw the man beneath the surplice. Kind. Loving. Vulnerable. I can't let her do this.

He deserves better than what she has planned for him. I can't go through with it. I won't. I couldn't bear to look in his eyes when he discovers he's been played for a fool. Don't want to see the hurt. Don't want him to see how much I'm hurting. It's better this way. Better that he never knows what I almost did. Let him remember me the way he saw me. As the girl he believed I could be.

The water is cold but I welcome its icy embrace and I give myself into its arms, smiling as they fold themselves around me and draw me close.

The Tale of the Baron

H.D.W. Loten

(originally published in "Twisted Tales – Makarelle')

A clear April sky.
Burning orange flames.
A plane swivels. It falls falls
falls from grace in an
inelegant tumble: it
twists and turns.

His adversary in the machine -
The King of the Air - twists
in a corkscrew.
Through the clouds. Turns
above the barren fields hunting
His next victim. Tossing his frame high.

Red as the blood of his prey,
His Lordship locks his target. Toils
behind him. A flurry. A flutter. Then
the spin begins. Round and
round: sparks swirl in a
great leaping flame.

Machines up high, rising into an arc,
Target in sight. Breath held.
The thrill of the kill.
It falters. It roils. Then
comes the gyrating fall to
the snaking trenches below him.

The fourth plane is downed
by The Baron in His Red Machine.
His name made. His legacy secured. Enough for one day.
The Squadron Leader's swivelling engines
and rotating propeller roll Him home
Bloody April's savage scourge.

His Flying Circus of Death entertains
the ranks on the ground as planes
pirouette in their domain.
A month of infamy and fear.
Enemies curl through His land up
high and He fells all that come before Him.

A clear April sky.
Burning Red flames.
His plane swivels. It falls falls
falls from grace in a final
inelegant tumble: he
twists and turns.

Gnarled remains of Reddened
burning wood and steel.
Ousted from his
throne, no longer King or Baron.
His twisted reign of eighty kills ends
with his own. His ruthless tale still swirls.

Twilight of Sanity
H.D.W. Loten

Fall of dusk is harsh.
I breathe in deeply,
ignore the chill down my spine.
I look at the men around me,
Burnie, Charlie, Roge, Hal.
They begin to shout…

A sharp stiff screech in my ears.
A train? no.
A scream? maybe.
A whistle? yes.
Up the ladder into
the endless brown and grey.
Bono, Conner, Richards, Haroldson.
So much death for one hole.

Last light is brightened by a rattle.
A machine-gun.
I stumble.
I collapse.
I close my eyes.
I cover my ears.
I roll onto my back.
Paralysis.
My ears ring.

The sky is clear,
bright blue light,
like colour on a painter's canvas.
It becomes dimmer.
Danker.
Dirtier.
Mud flies onto it.
The painter flicks paint on his work,
it ruins it.

I absorb every moment.

A massive roar.
A blackened roar.
A desperate roar.
A silenced scream.
It fills the empty sky,
swirls on the starry night.
The image crumbles before me.

Fifty yards.
Fifty yards.
Fifty yards.
That was it.
The painter has destroyed his art,
like Dorian Grey.
Grey.
Brown.
Red.

Empty. My soul is empty.
Burst like a dam.
Filled with a ruthless, raging cry.
Cry. Cry. Cry in anguish.
A strange land, new to my eyes,
Blurred.
Drenched.
Miserable.

Silence fills me.
The needle has been pulled,
torn from the gramophone.
Silence.
Silence has never been louder.
My ears ring…

Now there is a light.
Blinding, white in the sky.
It stings my eyes.
My ears ring…

Fall of dusk. All is gone.
Everything.
Everything.
Everything.
Except the will.
The will to draw breath.
The will.
My ears ring…

Rebellion

R.E. Loten

(originally published on the Shaftesbury Tree Festival website)

11 June 2015, Wyndham's Oak, Dorset

Emily leant back against the broad trunk of the tree, closed her eyes and breathed in deeply. Her father was always a proponent of the benefits of fresh air and she certainly needed them. She was waiting for Iain and he was late as usual. *He'll be with her again, no doubt. She'll have made an excuse to delay him.* There was always an excuse. Emily had known his reputation before they got together but she convinced herself she could change him. She would be different. She'd be the one to keep him. Instead, she spent their time apart wondering what *they* were doing. Whether he professed his love for her. Whether he was going to leave. Emily had made a decision though and told him they needed to talk. She was tired of being messed about.

Something brushed against her forehead and she swatted it away impatiently. *It would be just my luck to get a mosquito bite in the middle of my face today of all days. I've got to tell him that it's time to make his mind up. Her or me.* That's why she'd asked him to meet her by the tree. She'd been teaching her class about the Monmouth rebellion earlier that week and it had inspired her to be bold. They'd hung some of Monmouth's supporters on the very spot she was now sitting on, when the rebellion failed and she admired that they were willing to fight (and die in some cases) for what they wanted. For what they believed they were owed. She wanted to make a point. She and Iain had been together for two years now. She'd waited long enough.

Something brushed her face again. She opened her mouth as she swatted it away again. Then screamed. A pair of feet dangled in front of her face, the lace from the white socks encasing the legs must have been what had tickled her. Backing away in horror, she felt the rough bark of the trunk scratch her back through the thin sundress as she slid up the tree, unable to bear the thought of that *thing* touching her again. She moaned quietly as she realised her bag was still on the floor. Backing around the side of the tree, she stretched an arm out and groped blindly for the strap, pulling it towards her in relief as her fingers closed around the thin leather. Stumbling slightly, her feet catching on the uncut grass, she hurled herself away from the tree, the breath catching in her throat. Iain would have to think what he wanted when she wasn't there to meet him. She couldn't stay there, not in that place. Not with the ghost.

High in the branches of the tree, concealed by the broad swathe of foliage, Melissa stifled a giggle. *It was almost too easy*, she thought, as she hauled the dummy back into the tree. Iain had never been the most subtle of people and she'd found out about his wandering eye not long after their marriage. She stayed with him because of the children mainly, but this time he'd seemed different. She wasn't going to beg him to stay – quite the reverse actually, she'd packed his bags ready for when he got home later – but she was damned if she was going to let them get off scot-free. Putting the fear of God into Emily had been fun but it was almost too easy. For a teacher of history she was amazingly gullible and loved to see ghosts everywhere. (Melissa had discovered that little pearl of information via Iain's credit card statement – the ghost hunting trip certainly hadn't been purchased for her.) Melissa smiled grimly. *Oh yes*, she thought. *I've got far more fun planned for those two.*

Sat on a Trigpoint
H.D.W. Loten

Rolling hills that swept across the countryside,
dotted with blackened bushes.
Legions of thin dark green trees
stood to attention,
refusing to move with the wind.

Small rock formations
surrounded the crest
like a besieging army,
then on the near horizon,
mounds of earth thrust skyward.
Each dotted with small hamlets and
communities of stones, large rocks
and other forms of nature.

The hills bore rocks
like a tree bares fruit.
On the far horizon they
conjoined together to form,
a huge battlement when
combined with the distortion of hazy clouds
that swooped beneath the hilltops.

Farther below were the poorly labelled paths,
that rocked through the hills.
Following the base of the hill to the west,
piles of slated stones
created walls.
Here, cattle and sheep freely roamed.

Turning north, hedges, trees
and other bushes split the
mostly quadrilateral fields in twain.
Splitting them again were roads
that carried trucks and cars.

Facing the southern slope of Fox Tor,
a small calf lay sleeping,
covered by some shrubs,
and guarded by its mother's watchful eyes
that overlooked it nearer to the crest.

Printed in Great Britain
by Amazon

17562684R00032